For my boys, Eddie and Willie

Also published by Ruwanga Trading:
The Whale Who Wanted to be Small
The Wonderful Journey
A Whale's Tale
Gecko Hide and Seek
The Goodnight Gecko
The Brave Little Turtle
The Gift of Aloha
Tikki Turtle's Quest

BOOK ENQUIRIES AND ORDERS:
Booklines Hawaii, Ltd.
269 Pali'i Street
Mililani, Hawaii. 96789
Phone: (808) 676-0116
E-mail: bookline@lava.net

First published 1990 by Ruwanga Trading
ISBN 0-9615102-5-0
Printed in China through Everbest Printing Co., Ltd.

THE SHARK
who learned a lesson

written and illustrated by
Gill McBarnet

Ruwanga Trading

There was once a warm and sunlit coral reef. The creatures of the reef loved their bright and colorful home.

However . . .
. . . the coral reef dropped down into the shadowy depths of the ocean, and lurking in the murky shadows was a naughty shark.

The shark's name was Shadow, and he loved to scare and startle the creatures of the reef. He would suddenly shoot out of the shadows, and the creatures would always flee away, just as fast as they could flee.

What fun he had, being a bully!

The eels would slither away,
   the octopus would slink away.
The flying fish would fly away . . .
   and all the other little fish would flash away
   like jewels scattering in the bright blue water.

Whenever they saw Shadow,
   the dolphins would leap away.
The rays would glide away,
   the turtles would hide away . . .
   and all the little crabs would scuttle away
   behind the nearest rock.

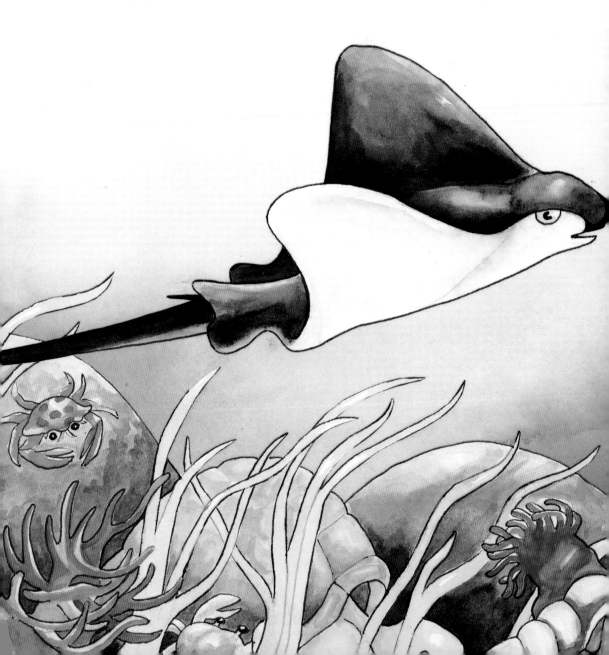

The creatures of the reef were jittery and scared, so one day when Shadow the shark was out cruising, Dippy the dolphin called a meeting.

"Shadow is always scaring us!" Complained a parrot fish.

"We don't like the way he sneaks up on us." Said an eel.

". . . and we're hardly getting any sleep." Yawned a turtle.

"I have an idea," said Dippy, and with that they put their heads and feelers and flippers and fins together, and decided how they would teach Shadow the shark a lesson. Then they went back to doing whatever they normally did, as if nothing had happened.

When Shadow returned, he was already looking for someone to scare ... such a bully was he! Slipping out of the shadows and into the reef, he chuckled because he loved seeing the creatures fleeing away from him.

"Ha, ha!" Said Shadow.

Just ahead of him were some little fish.
"The smaller they are, the more I can scare them," he snickered.

This time the little fish seemed to be waiting for him, but in a flash they turned and fled away together. Chuckling gleefully, Shadow sped after them.

Over coral and seaweed they swam and swam . . .

. . . with Shadow the shark just a snip and a snap behind them.

Into a shipwreck on the ocean bed ...

... and out through a porthole the little fish fled!
Closer and closer that naughty shark sped, when suddenly ...

"Oh, no!" Snarled Shadow, when he found he was stuck in the porthole. The little fish had slipped through easily, but Shadow was trapped when he tried to follow them.

"Come back!" He grumbled, annoyed that the fish had got away.

To the shark's surprise they DID come back ... and they were joined by all the other creatures of the reef. All those creatures he had bullied and chased for so long, were now moving menacingly towards HIM! Shadow had always thought they were timid and meek, but they didn't look timid now ... their eyes flashed angrily as they slithered, slunk, swam, leapt, crept and scuttled towards him.

Shadow wanted to flee away but he couldn't, he was stuck!

For the first time in his life he was scared, and he didn't like being scared at all.

"No! Leave me alone, you bullies!" He cried, terrified.

"We will only leave YOU alone, if you will leave US alone!"
Said Dippy the dolphin in his sternest voice.
"You must return to your home in the shadowy deep,
and promise not to bully us, ever again!" The dolphin commanded.
"I promise, I promise . . ." whimpered the terrified shark, who was
really nothing but a coward at heart.
"Help me get out of here!" Wailed Shadow, whose only wish now,
was to be as far away from the reef as possible.

So the dolphin pushed.
The ray and eel and octopus pushed.
The hermit crab and dainty starfish pushed . . .
    and all the little fishes of the reef came to help push
    Shadow the shark out of the shipwreck, and away from the reef

The minute he was free from the porthole, Shadow the shark turned and swam away from the reef as fast as he could swim. He wanted to get away from the seaweed that tickled him, the coral that clawed at him . . . and all the little creatures who were slinking, slithering, swimming, leaping, creeping and scuttling after him. His fins flipped and flapped in his fluster to flee the reef . . .

. . . and that was the last time they were ever bothered by Shadow the shark.

The warm and sunlit coral reef is now a pleasant place to be. The creatures of the reef can eat and sleep and play in peace and harmony.

As for Shadow the shark ... he's learned a good lesson. He found out what it is like to be scared, so he will now think twice about bullying those who seem timid and meek!